D0605170
WITHDRAWN

dream jobs™

I want to be a MOVIE STAR

Katie Franks

Published in 2007 by The Rosen Publishing Group, Inc.
29 East 21st Street, New York, NY 10010

First Edition

Editor: Jennifer Way
Book Design: Ginny Chu
Photo Researchers: Sam Cha and Ginny Chu

Photo Credits: All Photos © Getty Images.

Library of Congress Cataloging-in-Publication Data

Franks, Katie.
I want to be a movie star / Katie Franks. — 1st ed.
p. cm. — (Dream jobs)
Includes index.
ISBN-13: 978-1-4042-3619-6 (library binding)
ISBN-10: 1-4042-3619-8 (library binding)
1. Motion pictures—Juvenile literature. 2. Motion picture actors and actresses—Juvenile literature. I. Title.
PN1994.5.F75 2007
791.43—dc22
2006019458

Manufactured in the United States of America

Contents

Movie Stars 5
Working on Movie Sets 7
Making Movies 9
Going to Movie Premieres 11
Meeting Fans 13
The Walk of Fame 15
Doing Charity Work 17
Directing Movies 19
Winning an Oscar 21
Becoming a Legend 22
Glossary 23
Index 24
Web Sites 24

Kirsten Dunst and Orlando Bloom are two young movie stars. Dunst has appeared in *Bring It On*. Bloom has appeared in the Pirates of the Caribbean movies.

Movie Stars

Do you have a favorite actor or actress? Do you love going to the movies? You might dream about having an acting **career**. Maybe you also like to learn more about movie stars' lives. There are many things movie stars do in addition to acting in **films**. This book will show you just a few of the things that make up this dream job.

Here is Tobey Maguire and the director Sam Raimi.
They are on the set of *Spider-Man*.

Working on Movie Sets

Movies are filmed on sets. Sometimes the sets are places that have been built just for that film at the movie **studio**. When actors get to a set, they work with many people. These can be the people who work on the actors' **costumes** and people who do the actors' hair and makeup. Actors also work with the director, who helps them **rehearse** their parts. The director is also the person who films the movie.

Russell Crowe learned how to sword fight for *Gladiator*. This movie was filmed on location in Malta.

Making Movies

Sometimes a movie is filmed on location. This means that the movie is filmed somewhere that is not at a movie studio. For example, the Lord of the Rings movies were filmed on location in New Zealand. Sometimes movie stars need to work with special coaches to learn skills for their part in a movie. Some of these skills might be singing, dancing, playing music, horseback riding, and sword fighting.

Daniel Radcliffe, Emma Watson, and Rupert Grint star in the Harry Potter movies. Here they are in 2005, at the premiere of *Harry Potter and the Goblet of Fire*.

Going to Movie Premieres

Movie stars also help **promote** movies they are in. There are many ways movie stars do this. They can go on talk shows on TV. They can talk to reporters, who will then write articles about the star and the movie. They may also go to the movie's **premiere**. Movie stars can talk to fans and reporters as they enter the premiere. This is known as walking the **red carpet**.

Christian Bale is signing autographs at a premiere of *Batman Begins*.

Meeting Fans

Movie stars have many chances to meet their fans. They can meet fans at movie premieres or at other special times. It can be very **exciting** for people to meet their favorite movie stars. A fan might like to tell a movie star how much they enjoy watching their films. Many people like to get movie stars' **autographs**. Some people like to have their picture taken with their favorite movie star.

In 2006, Queen Latifah received a star on the Walk of Fame in Hollywood, California.

The Walk of Fame

Another fun thing that movie stars may get to do is receive a star on the Walk of Fame. The Walk of Fame is in Hollywood, California. The stars along the walk honor people who work in movies, TV, **theater**, radio, and music. The stars are given to people who have been chosen by fans. To get a star, the person must also have done well in their career and helped out the community.

Angelina Jolie works for the United Nations. Here she is in Pakistan after an earthquake. An earthquake is the shaking of Earth's surface.

Doing Charity Work

Many movie stars like to do **charity** work in their free time. Sometimes movie stars can use the attention that is given to them to bring attention to their favorite charities. This can help the charity raise money. It can also help bring greater attention to a problem. For example, Lucy Liu works with UNICEF, a charity that helps poor children around the world.

George Clooney has received attention and honors for the films he has directed.

Directing Movies

Some movie stars like to do other jobs in film besides acting. They may start a production company. A production company is a business that chooses movies and works to get those movies made. Drew Barrymore has a production company called Flower Films. Many movie stars also like to direct movies. Robert Redford, Salma Hayek, and Denzel Washington are just a few movie stars who have also directed movies.

In 2006, Reese Witherspoon won an Oscar for her performance in the movie *Walk the Line*.

Winning an Oscar

The Academy Awards, or Oscars, are held each year. Oscars are given to movie stars for their accomplishments in acting. You can watch the Oscars on TV and see if your favorite movie stars win an award. Winning an Academy Award is one of the greatest honors for a movie star. When movie stars win Oscars, they can feel proud about their **performance** in a film.

Becoming a Legend

After a long career in the movies, some movie stars are called **legends**. A movie star who is a legend has made many well-loved movies. A legend may have a star on the Walk of Fame or may have won an Oscar. Audrey Hepburn, Meryl Streep, Robert DeNiro, and Morgan Freeman are a few examples of movie stars who are thought of as legends.

Glossary

autographs (AH-toh-grafs) People's names, written by those people.
career (kuh-REER) A job.
charity (CHER-uh-tee) A group that gives help to the needy.
costumes (kos-TOOMZ) Clothes worn by an actor in a film.
exciting (ik-SY-ting) Very interesting.
films (FILMZ) Movies.
legends (LEH-jendz) People who have been famous and honored for a very long time.
performance (per-FOR-ments) Singing, dancing, acting, or playing music in front of other people.
premiere (prih-MEER) The first showing of a movie.
promote (pruh-MOHT) To raise attention about something.
red carpet (RED KAR-pet) The walkway that leads to the building where something special is happening. This walkway is generally covered with a red carpet.
rehearse (rih-HERS) To practice something.
studio (STOO-dee-oh) A building where movie sets are made. A studio can also be the place where a movie company runs its business.
theater (THEE-uh-tur) The live art in which people put on plays.

Index

A
autographs, 13

C
costumes, 7

D
director, 7

F
fans, 11, 13, 15

M
movie studio, 7, 9

O
Oscar(s), 21–22

P
premiere(s), 11, 13
production company, 19

R
red carpet, 11

S
sets, 7

T
talk shows, 11

W
Walk of Fame, 15

Web Sites

Due to the changing nature of Internet links, PowerKids Press has developed an online list of Web sites related to the subject of this book. This site is updated regularly. Please use this link to access the list:
www.powerkidslinks.com/djobs/movie/